• Louanne Pig in •

WITCH LADY

Nancy Carlson

Puffin Books

To all my friends
from the old neighborhood

GNV

PUFFIN BOOKS
Viking Penguin Inc., 40 West 23rd Street,
New York, New York 10010, U.S.A.
Penguin Books Ltd, Harmondsworth, Middlesex, England
Penguin Books Australia Ltd, Ringwood, Victoria, Australia
Penguin Books Canada Limited, 2801 John Street,
Markham, Ontario, Canada L3R 1B4
Penguin Books (N.Z.) Ltd, 182–190 Wairau Road,
Auckland 10, New Zealand

First published by Carolrhoda Books Inc. 1985
Published in Picture Puffins 1986
Copyright © Nancy Carlson, 1985
All rights reserved
Printed in U.S.A. by General Offset, Jersey City, New Jersey
Set in Bookman

Library of Congress Cataloging in Publication Data
Carlson, Nancy L.   Louanne Pig in witch lady.
Summary: Louanne Pig is befriended by the old woman she
always believed to be a witch.
[1. Friendship—Fiction.   2. Pigs—Fiction]   I. Title.
[PZ7.C21665L1   1986]   [E]   86-3250   ISBN 0-14-050602-0

WITCH LADY

Everyone knew that the house on top of the
hill belonged to a witch.

George had seen her black cat.

Ralph had heard her screeching at the children she tortured.

Harriet had once been brave enough to peek through her dining room window.

"There were tall cages everywhere," she told
her friends. "She must be fattening up an awful
lot of kids."

Still, every now and then it was fun to cut
through the witch lady's yard.

It made them all feel very brave indeed.

One windy October day, the four friends
decided to prove their courage once again.

They were almost over the fence and safe
when Louanne tripped.

"Owww!" she cried. "I've twisted my ankle.
I can't stand up!"

George and Ralph and Harriet thought about
going back to help their friend . . .

. . . but just as they got up their courage, the witch lady appeared.

"You naughty children!" she yelled at them.
"Scat!" She clapped her hands.

George and Ralph and Harriet didn't think
twice. They ran like lightning.

The witch lady looked down at Louanne.
"What's wrong with *you*?" she asked. "Be off
with you!"

"I . . . uh . . . I . . . uh . . . I . . . ," Louanne stuttered.
"Spit it out, child," scolded the witch lady.
"I can't," Louanne finally blurted out. "I've twisted my ankle."

"Oh, dear," sighed the witch lady. "Well, I can't fix it out here in the cold. There's nothing for it but to come inside."

Louanne knew her goose was really cooked
now, but she had no choice.

The witch lady helped her hobble up the
steps and into the living room.

"Sit here," she said, "while I boil some water."

Oh, no, thought Louanne. She's going to boil
me alive.

Soon the witch lady returned with a plate of cookies and a cup of tea.

Fattening me up for the kill, thought Louanne.

Then she wrapped cold cloths around Louanne's ankle. In a little while it felt much better.

"Would you like to see my house?" the witch lady asked. Louanne nodded. She was beginning to think they might have been wrong about her.

Upstairs the black cat was curled up in the
sun.

"His name is Figaro," said the witch lady. "Go
ahead and pet him." Louanne did. Figaro began
to purr. "He likes you," said the witch lady.

In the dining room were six tall cages. There
were no children locked up in them, though.
They were filled with birds.

"Ohhh," sighed Louanne. "They're beautiful."

Before Louanne left, the witch lady played the piano and sang for her. It did sound a little like screeching.

When Louanne got home, she found George
and Harriet and Ralph on her front steps.

"You're alive!" yelled Harriet.
"How did you ever escape?" asked George.
"You're so brave!" said Ralph.

"I guess I am pretty brave," said Louanne.
"In fact, I'm *so* brave, I think I just might go
back there tomorrow...

I forgot to ask her name!"